D1471269

ROMANS BY ANN JUNGMAN & MIKE PHILLIPS

Bacillus and the Beastly Bath
Clottus and the Ghostly Gladiator
Tertius and the Horrible Hunt
Twitta and the Ferocious Fever

First paperback edition 2002
First published 2002 in hardback by
A & C Black (Publishers) Ltd
37 Soho Square, London W1D 3QZ

ISBN 0-7136-5963-7

A CIP catalogue record for this book is available
from the British Library.

Printed and bound by G. Z. Printek, Bilbao, Spain.

ROMANS

Tertius
and the
Horrible Hunt

ANN JUNGMAN

ILLUSTRATED BY
MIKE PHILLIPS

A & C BLACK • LONDON

CHAPTER 1

The Unexpected Letter

'Letter from Rome, letter all the way from Rome itself!' shouted Bacillus.

'Let me see!' cried Clottus.

'It's not for you, it's for the master,' replied Bacillus. 'I have to give it directly to him and no one else.'

Just then Marcellus rode in on his horse.

'Master, master, I have a letter for you, all the way from Rome itself,' said Bacillus, running over to his master.

Clottus put his foot out by mistake and Bacillus tripped straight over it. He fell flat on his face in the mud.

'Watch it!' shouted Marcellus. 'Idiot, you'll get it all covered in mud. If I can't read this important letter, you'll get a good whipping.'

Marcellus opened the scroll and read what was on it.

'Oh! Well, well! What do you know!'

'Father, what does the letter say?'
demanded Clottus.

'Oh no! Well that's the last thing I expected.
What a surprise!'

'What's a surprise?' nagged Clottus, jumping up and trying to read over his father's shoulder.

'Wonders will never cease,' Marcellus went on as he folded the letter. 'The things that happen in this life. You never know what to prepare for.'

'Father, I am dying of curiosity. What is going on?'

'Oh, just that my brother Severus is coming to take over command of the garrison at Chester and wants to leave your cousin Tertius here with us.'

'You mean, someone from Rome is coming to live in our house?' asked Clottus.

'That's right,' said Marcellus. 'Ah, it will be so good to see some family again. You know, I often think the worst thing about being part of a great empire is that so many of us end up far from home and our families.'

Marcellus put his arm round his son. 'Come on, Clottus, we'll go and tell your mother and Twitta the good news. Bacillus, go and bathe and change.'

'Yes master,' sighed Bacillus, as father and son walked into the house together.

Deleria and Twitta were delighted by the news.

'It will be so wonderful to see dear Severus and Caterpilla again,' said Deleria, smiling. 'And it will be lovely for you children to have a chance to get to know your cousin. Oh, Marcellus, this is the best news you could have brought me.'

'Don't get too excited, Deleria. They won't be here for several weeks,' said her husband.

'That's just as well, because I'll have to get the house cleaned from top to bottom and I think we should get some fresh murals painted on the walls and some new couches for the dining room.'

'I'm sure none of that is necessary, my dear.'

'I'm sure it is, Marcellus,' argued his wife. 'After all, we don't want them thinking that we have forgotten our manners or that we don't have any style here in Britain, do we?'

'Well, no need to overdo it. I'm not made of money, you know. We can't compete with Rome, my love, no matter what we do.'

CHAPTER 2

Home Improvements

For weeks, workmen swarmed through the house. All the floors were dug up so that a more efficient heating system could be installed.

'This is even worse than I expected,' complained Marcellus. 'Why can't they take us as they find us?'

In the dining room artists stood on high trestles painting new murals.

'Clottus,' said his mother, 'under no circumstances are you to go anywhere near the dining room, do you understand?'

'I don't see why not,' grumbled Clottus, 'I want to see what's going on.'

'You know there tend to be accidents when you're around, Clottus. Now, the house has got to look really good when your aunt and uncle and cousin arrive from Rome.'

'Not fair,' moaned Clottus.

The next day, Twitta stood looking at the mural with her cloak over her face.

'Hello, Mistress Twitta,' said one of the painters, 'I'm surprised to see you here again so soon. You were only in this morning.'

Twitta muttered something into her cloak and she gazed at the wonderful new coloured pictures that were taking shape on the walls.

Just then, Deleria ran in. 'Have any of you seen Master Clottus? He's disappeared. Oh hello, Twitta, have you seen your twin brother?'

'Er — no,' Twitta mumbled, burying her head further in the cloak.

'Just a minute, Twitta! I saw you in the garden a minute ago. Clottus! You come here, this minute.'

Clottus threw off the cloak and tried to run away from his mother, but he ran straight into the trestle frame.

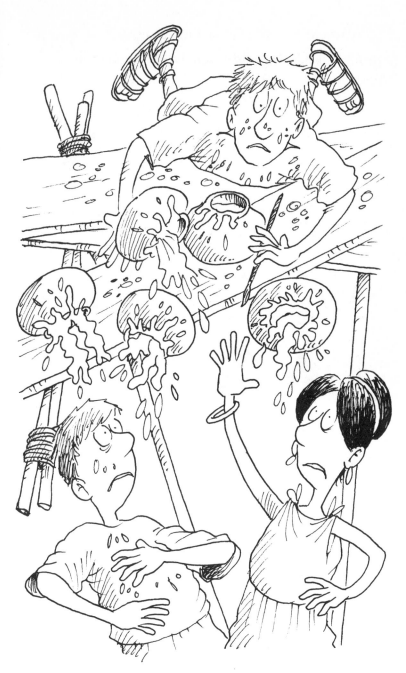

'You clumsy Clottus!' Deleria and the painter yelled as they sprawled on the floor covered in paint.

'It wasn't my fault,' said Clottus.

When the dining room was finished and the new couches and tables had been moved in, Deleria ordered the building of a bigger bath house with mosaic tiles all around.

The best mosaic layers came from Londinium and set to work. Clottus and Twitta watched them create lovely floors with beautiful patterns.

Deleria looked on proudly. 'We'll have the best mosaic floors and decoration in Britain,' she said. 'Won't the neighbours be impressed — to say nothing of our Roman visitors!'

'Can we make a mosaic, Mother?' asked Twitta.

'Don't be ridiculous,' replied her mother.

'But it looks fun,' said Clottus.

'The answer is No, Clottus, and it will continue to be No, whatever you say.'

'We'll sneak down at night,' Clottus whispered to Twitta.

So that night, as everyone slept, they crept downstairs and lit candles.

'What shall we make?' asked Twitta.

'A dog,' suggested Clottus.

'Good idea,' agreed Twitta, 'I'll do the head, you do the tail.'

'No, I want to do the head,' said Clottus. 'If I can't do the head, I'm going to bed.'

'Let's do an imaginary dog with two heads then,' said Twitta.

So they worked all night and made a big black dog with two heads.

In the morning the workmen were shocked and poor Deleria fainted.

Twitta and Clottus were beaten for being so disobedient.

'It was worth it, though, wasn't it, Twitta?' sniffed Clottus.

'Definitely,' she moaned back.

CHAPTER 3

Visitors

'When are the visitors from Rome coming?' asked Twitta.

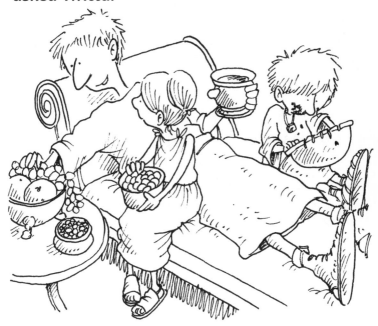

'We're not quite sure. Within the week, I imagine,' replied her father. 'It depends how long they spend in Londinium and then how long it takes them to get here. I've sent Gorjus into Verulamium with instructions to ride back here like the wind and tell us as soon as he spots them.'

'How will he recognise them?' demanded Clottus.

'Well, there aren't that many strange generals from Rome passing through our little town,' said Marcellus.

Just then they heard the sound of a horse galloping towards the house.

'It's Gorjus!' yelled Clottus, and they all rushed to the door.

'They're here, sir!' Gorjus gasped. 'Just coming up from town, sir. They should arrive in about half an hour.'

'Thank you, Gorjus. Go and get Perpendicula to give you some refreshments. Twitta, go and tell your mother.'

Twitta burst into her mother's room.
Deleria was having her hair done in a very
elaborate style by two slaves.

'They're going to be here in half an hour,'
Twitta informed her.

'Hurry up, you stupid creatures,' snapped
Deleria to the slaves. 'You've got ten minutes
to finish. Twitta, go and get my jewel box.'

While Deleria put on as many jewels as she could find room for, she ordered the slaves to do something with Twitta's hair.

'Do I have to?' groaned Twitta.

'Yes, you do. I want you to be a credit to me.'

'Ouch!' said Twitta as the slaves put the finishing touches to her new hairstyle. Deleria looked at her daughter. 'Now you can wear this lovely brooch and this wonderful piece in your hair.' She helped Twitta put them on. 'You look much better, a daughter to be proud of!'

Twitta felt self-conscious, but Deleria was
very excited. 'Come along, now! We must all
be at the door to greet them.'

The whole family and all the slaves lined up
in the courtyard. In the distance they could
hear a carriage lumbering towards the villa.

The carriage came under the arch and into the courtyard.

Coughing and spluttering, a woman and a boy climbed out first.

'Deleria, my dear!' cried the woman. 'How do you stand it, that road, all the dust? Oh dear, oh dear!'

The boy said nothing.

Then Severus climbed down from his horse and embraced his brother. 'Marcellus, how excellent to see you! I don't expect you'll recognise Caterpilla and our son Tertius after all these years.'

'No, indeed! Welcome, welcome to you all. You know Deleria already, but these two are the terrible twins, Clottus and Twitta, whom you have never met.'

'Welcome, Uncle and Aunt. Welcome, cousin Tertius,' chorused the twins. Still the boy said nothing.

'And how was your journey?' asked Marcellus.

'Don't ask,' shrieked Caterpilla. 'We've never been so bumped and thrown about! How you stand these British roads, I do not know. I mean, the ones our Roman boys built are fine, of course, but once you leave the main road it's unspeakable.'

'Come in and have a rest,' suggested Deleria. 'Bacillus will show you to your quarters. You can change and rest and then come down for a bath.'

'Oh, what a sweet little house,' said Caterpilla.

'It's the biggest house for miles around!' cried Marcellus.

'Well yes, by British standards I expect it is quite large, but when one has known Rome very recently, it seems modest, very modest.'

Later, Deleria took Caterpilla to see the brand new bath house.

'We've just had it installed,' Deleria explained proudly.

'Oh, what a dinky little bath house!' cried Caterpilla. 'Severus, come here and look, it's so sweet! Come and see Deleria's pride and joy. Oh, how our friends in Rome would laugh if they saw this place!'

Twitta and Clottus looked at each other. Twitta somehow managed to sneeze, and fell against Clottus. Clottus fell against Caterpilla...

...and there was a loud splash.

Clottus and Twitta went to bed without any supper.

CHAPTER 4

Tertius

The next morning Clottus and Twitta stood in front of their father.

'How could you behave like that? And to my brother's wife! I'm ashamed of both of you.'

'But Father, it was an accident,' explained Twitta. 'We didn't mean to push Caterpilla into the bath.'

'We really didn't mean to, Father,' agreed Clottus, 'and you know how clumsy I am.'

'Well, today I am expecting you to make up for it and entertain your cousin Tertius. It's hard for him being in a new country and I want you to be nice and kind. Is that clear?'

'Yes, Father,' chorused the twins.

'And if I find that you haven't looked after him properly, tonight you will go to bed hungry *and* get a beating.' So they went and found Tertius.

'Tertius,' said Clottus, trying to be friendly, 'would you like to come and see the farm? I've got two dogs, who are just wonderful.'

'And I've got a cat called Platia, and she's just had the most lovely kittens,' added Twitta.

'No thanks,' mumbled Tertius. 'They would just remind me of my animals that I've had to leave at home.'

'Then let's play five stones,' suggested Clottus. 'I bet you play that in Rome.'

'Not much,' sniffed Tertius.

'Well then, marbles. I've got some terrific marbles here, Tertius, look,' said Clottus kindly. 'In fact, you can choose the five that you like best and I'll give them to you.'

'I've got my own marbles,' Tertius told them. 'Roman ones, much better than yours.'

So they played marbles and deliberately let Tertius win but he still looked miserable.

'What's up with you, Tertius?' asked Twitta. 'Don't you ever smile?'

'Yes,' sniffed Tertius. 'In Rome I do, all the time. But I hate it here.'

'Why?' demanded the twins.

'It's horrible, it's cold and it's wet and I don't know anyone and I had to leave all my friends and pets behind.'

'Poor Tertius,' said Twitta.

'It must be tough having to move just because of your father's job,' agreed Clottus. 'But really, this is a wonderful place to live, Tertius. What can we do to make you see that?'

'I know,' shouted Twitta, 'hunting! Father and Gorjus say we have the best hunting here in the whole Roman Empire. The woods are full of deer and wild boar and even wolves and bears. Do you like riding and hunting, Tertius?'

A grin spread over Tertius's face. 'Oh yes, I love hunting. It's my favourite thing. Could you lend me a good, lively horse, Clottus?'

'No problem there,' said Clottus. 'Come on, we'll go to the stables now and get Gorjus to choose you a horse.'

'We'll give the dogs a run at the same time.'

'Last one to the stables is a smelly goat!'

CHAPTER 5

The Horrible Hunt

The next day Marcellus, Severus, Gorjus,
Tertius and Clottus set off at dawn.

'You have a good seat on a horse for a Roman,' Gorjus told Tertius. Tertius looked pleased and galloped off ahead.

'Come back!' shouted his father. 'You don't know this country at all. Tertius, stay by us. None of your wild ways today.'

Tertius slowed up a little.

'So you're going to Chester,' commented Gorjus to Severus. 'It's much wetter and colder there than here, you know.'

'Nonsense,' laughed Severus.

'It's true,' argued Marcellus, 'and the people up there, they all go around naked and painted blue.'

'That's right,' said Gorjus, 'and they eat people. Roasted Roman is their favourite dish!'

'And the dogs up there have two heads like the one in our mosaic,' added Clottus.

'A likely tale,' said Severus grinning.

They all laughed as they approached the thick forest.

'Everyone stay together,' said Gorjus. 'Follow me and keep my red headband in sight. This is a very large and thick forest — it's all too easy to get lost. So, beware!'

They were trotting along when suddenly a wild boar rushed at them from the undergrowth. They managed to ride away, all except Tertius.

'All right boar,' shouted Tertius bravely. 'This is a Roman you're dealing with! Prepare to meet your death!'

The boar snorted and then charged Tertius, whose horse panicked and threw him.

Quickly, Tertius picked up his spear and aimed it at the boar — but missed. The boar was getting angry and he charged Tertius again.

Tertius climbed a tree but not before the boar scraped his foot with his tusk and injured him.

The boar walked round the tree making a terrible snorting noise.

'I shall be stuck up here for ever,' wept Tertius, as it began to rain. Then it poured. Then there was thunder and lightning, followed by hail.

'Help,' shouted Tertius, 'I'm over here!' He knew no one would hear him.

Suddenly the boar keeled over. Tertius peered down at it.

'How clever I am,' thought Tertius. 'I must have tired it out and now it's died from exhaustion. I killed a wild boar, all on my own!'

He cheered up a bit and climbed down from the tree.

As Tertius stood by the dead boar, wondering what to do next, a woodcutter came out of the forest.

'You must be lost,' said the woodcutter.

'I am,' said Tertius, 'but I'm a Roman and I can look after myself. Look, I just killed this boar!'

'Indeed?' said the woodcutter, hiding his bow and arrow behind his back. 'Come on, young master, you'll be living with Marcellus, I'll be bound. Let's get you home.'

So Tertius was returned to his family, who were all in a terrible state not knowing what had happened to him.

'I told you not to go off and do your own thing,' yelled Severus. 'We've been going mad with worry.'

'But I killed a boar all on my own, on foot,' Tertius told them.

'Well, you shouldn't have tried it,' Gorjus told him, 'you might have been killed!'

'My baby!' said Caterpilla, and fainted.

But Marcellus congratulated his nephew. 'Well done, Tertius! Come on, Gorjus! Let's go and find this boar and tonight we'll have a feast.'

That night they all enjoyed a wonderful banquet and everyone agreed that maybe there was something to be said for living in Britain after all.